Dear Parents and Educators,

Welcome to Penguin Young Readers! As parent[s], [we] know that each child develops at his or her own pace—in terms of speech, critical thinking, and, of course, reading. Penguin Young Readers recognizes this fact. As a result, each Penguin Young Readers book is assigned a traditional easy-to-read level (1–4) as well as a Guided Reading Level (A–P). Both of these systems will help you choose the right book for your child. Please refer to the back of each book for specific leveling information. Penguin Young Readers features esteemed authors and illustrators, stories about favorite characters, fascinating nonfiction, and more!

Fox Outfoxed

LEVEL **3**

GUIDED
READING
LEVEL **J**

This book is perfect for a **Transitional Reader** who:
- can read multisyllable and compound words;
- can read words with prefixes and suffixes;
- is able to identify story elements (beginning, middle, end, plot, setting, characters, problem, solution); and
- can understand different points of view.

Here are some **activities** you can do during and after reading this book:
- The title of this story is *Fox Outfoxed*. The word *outfoxed* means outsmarted. Discuss what it means to be outfoxed, or outsmarted. Then discuss how Fox was outfoxed in each chapter of this book.
- Vocabulary: Some of the words in this story, like *outfoxed*, may be unfamiliar. Find the following words in the story, and then write down the definitions on a separate sheet of paper. Make sure the definition you find matches the way in which the word is used in this story.

clever	mind	serious	smug	tagging
gang	nick	shame	spree	ugly

Remember, sharing the love of reading with a child is the best gift you can give!

—Bonnie Bader, EdM
    Penguin Young Readers program

*Penguin Young Readers are leveled by independent reviewers applying the standards developed by Irene Fountas and Gay Su Pinnell in *Matching Books to Readers: Using Leveled Books in Guided Reading*, Heinemann, 1999.

For my sister, Cynthia

Penguin Young Readers
Published by the Penguin Group
Penguin Group (USA) Inc., 375 Hudson Street, New York, New York 10014, USA
Penguin Group (Canada), 90 Eglinton Avenue East, Suite 700, Toronto, Ontario M4P 2Y3, Canada
(a division of Pearson Penguin Canada Inc.)
Penguin Books Ltd., 80 Strand, London WC2R 0RL, England
Penguin Group Ireland, 25 St. Stephen's Green, Dublin 2, Ireland (a division of Penguin Books Ltd.)
Penguin Group (Australia), 250 Camberwell Road, Camberwell, Victoria 3124, Australia
(a division of Pearson Australia Group Pty. Ltd.)
Penguin Books India Pvt. Ltd., 11 Community Centre, Panchsheel Park, New Delhi—110 017, India
Penguin Group (NZ), 67 Apollo Drive, Rosedale, Auckland 0632, New Zealand
(a division of Pearson New Zealand Ltd.)
Penguin Books (South Africa) (Pty.) Ltd., 24 Sturdee Avenue,
Rosebank, Johannesburg 2196, South Africa

Penguin Books Ltd., Registered Offices: 80 Strand, London WC2R 0RL, England

Copyright © 1992 by James Marshall. All rights reserved. First published in 1992 by Dial Books for Young Readers, an imprint of Penguin Group (USA) Inc. Published in a Puffin Easy-to-Read edition in 1996. Published in 2012 by Penguin Young Readers, an imprint of Penguin Group (USA) Inc., 345 Hudson Street, New York, New York 10014. Manufactured in China.

The Library of Congress has catalogued the Dial edition
under the following Control Number: 91021815

ISBN 978-0-14-038113-9   10 9 8 7 6 5 4 3 2 1

FOX OUTFOXED

by James Marshall

Penguin Young Readers
An Imprint of Penguin Group (USA) Inc.

One Saturday morning

Fox went out for some fun.

At Carmen's house

something was up.

"The Big Race is today,"

said Carmen.

Fox looked at Carmen's race car.

"Does it have an engine?" he said.

"It has pedals," said Carmen.

"That's no fun," said Fox.

"First prize in The Big Race

is a free shopping spree

at the candy store," said Carmen.

Fox ran home to build

his own race car.

"There isn't much time," he said.

"May I help?" asked Louise.

"Go away," said Fox.

Then Fox had one of his great ideas.

He ran after Louise.

"You can help," said Fox.

"But you must do as I say."

"Oh goody!" said Louise.

Fox made it to the starting line
just in the nick of time.
He looked smug.

"On your mark!" cried the starter.

"Get set!

Go!"

The race was on!

Fox shot ahead of the others.

He was really moving!

He crossed the finish line.

But he kept right on going . . .

smack into Mrs. O'Hara's

pretty flower garden.

"You!" said Mrs. O'Hara.

"It wasn't my fault!"

said Fox.

Suddenly, out popped Louise.

"Did I run fast enough, Fox?"

she said.

"Aha!" yelled the starter.

"Shame, shame!" cried the others.

Fox spent the rest of the day
working in Mrs. O'Hara's garden.
"I hope you learned your lesson,"
said Dexter.
But Fox was in no mood to hear *that*.

COMIC
FOX

Fox had lots and lots
of comic books.

"Are you sure you have enough?"
said Mom.

"I could always use more,"
said Fox.

"I wasn't serious," said Mom.

"I couldn't live without my comics,"
said Fox.

And he took his 10 best comics
to read in the yard.

"This is great," said Fox.

Just then his pretty new neighbor,

Lulu, came by.

"May I see?" she said.

"Sure," said Fox.

"You don't read *comics*!" said Lulu.

"They're for little kids."

"Er . . . they're not mine," said Fox.

"I just found them.

I was about to throw them away."

"Then you won't mind if I take them for my little brother," said Lulu.

"Er . . . ," said Fox.

"Bye-bye," said Lulu.

And she was gone.

"My 10 best comics!" cried Fox.

He felt sick all afternoon.

Later he went for a walk.

In front of Lulu's house

he couldn't believe his eyes.

Lulu was reading Fox's comics
out loud to her friends.

"These are great!"
said her friends.

"Wait until you hear *this* one!"
said Lulu.

"It's my favorite!"

"Where did you get these?"
said her friends.

"Oh," said Lulu,

"I was *very* clever."

Fox had to go home and lie down.

"Is he dying?" said Louise.

"No," said Mom.

"But he's taking it pretty hard."

FOX
OUTFOXED

Halloween was coming up.

Fox and the gang were excited.

"My costume will be really wild!"

said Carmen.

"Think of all the tricks we can pull,"

said Dexter.

"Keep your voices down,"

whispered Fox.

"We don't want any little kids

tagging along."

On Halloween, Fox was ready.

He had worked hard on his costume.

"No one will ever know me," he said.

"Fox, dear," said Mom,

"Louise is all set

to go trick-or-treating."

"You're not serious!" said Fox.

"She'll just get in the way,

and her costume is *dumb*!"

"You're so mean," said Mom.

Carmen and Dexter were waiting.

"Mom made me bring Louise," said Fox.

"Little kids are trouble," said Dexter.

"I'll handle this," said Carmen.

"Now see here!" she said to Louise.

"Tonight I have magic powers.

Do not cause any problems.

Or I'll turn you into a *real* pumpkin!"

Louise didn't say a word.

"Little kids will believe *anything*,"

whispered Carmen to Fox.

They set off trick-or-treating.

Soon Dexter had an ugly thought.

"Little kids always get

the most treats," he said,

"and there won't be enough for us."

"Hmm," said Carmen.

At the corner of Cedar and Oak

they put Louise on a bench.

"Now don't you move," said Fox.

"We'll be right back."

And Louise was left all alone.

Fox and the gang went

to Mrs. O'Hara's house.

"Trick or treat!" they called out.

"Hello, Fox," said Mrs. O'Hara.

"I'd know *you* anywhere.

But where is your little sister?"

"Oh, she's around," said Fox.

Fox and the gang

went on trick-or-treating

until their bags were full.

"Let's go get Louise," said Fox.

They went back to the bench.

"Come on, Louise," said Fox.

But Louise didn't move.

"Come on, Louise!"

said Dexter and Carmen.

But Louise didn't budge.

"Oh my gosh!" cried Fox.

"It's a *real* pumpkin!"

"Wow!" said Carmen.

They went to the cops.

"My little sister got turned into

a pumpkin!" cried Fox.

"But it wasn't my fault!"

"Well, well," said Officer Bob.

"Maybe we could bake a nice pie."

"This is serious!" cried Fox.

"*Do* something!"

"I'm afraid it's too late,"

said Officer Bob.

Fox and the gang

left the police station.

On the way home

Fox tripped on his costume.

"Look out!" cried Carmen.

Fox went flying.

The pumpkin landed with a splat.

"Now you've done it!" said Dexter.

"Poor Louise," said Carmen.

"What a mess."

Fox put the pieces into a shopping bag
and ran to the hospital.

"Put Louise back together!" he cried.

"*Really,* Fox!" said Nurse Wendy.

"I don't have time for your jokes.

I've got a lot of sick people here."

Fox went home.

"Sit down, Mom," he said.

And he told her about Louise.

"That *is* too bad," said Mom.

"You're not cross?" said Fox.

"These things happen," said Mom.

"And we don't really *need* Louise."

"Don't say that!" cried Fox.

"She was always in the way,"
said Mom.

"Not always," said Fox.

"Would you be sweet to Louise
if we had her back?" said Mom.

"Oh, *yes*!" said Fox.

"I would even let her read my comics."

Louise flew out of the closet.

"Tra la!" she sang.

Fox nearly fainted.

"I get to read your comics!"
said Louise.

Later Fox heard Mom
and Louise talking.
"Fox really thought I turned into
a pumpkin!" said Louise.
"Big kids will believe *anything*!"

Fox went to bed very cross.

Mom came to say good night.

"I wasn't really fooled," said Fox.

"I was just playing along."

"You're so smart," said Mom.